The Berenstain Bears
Gifts of the Spirit
Fair Is Fair

Mike Berenstain

Based on the characters created by
Stan and Jan Berenstain

Random House 🏠 **New York**

To: _____

From: _____

"Show kindness and mercy to
one another."
—Zechariah 7:9

Copyright © 2022 by Berenstain Publishing, Inc. All rights reserved. Published in the United States by
Random House Children's Books, a division of Penguin Random House LLC, New York. Random House and
the colophon are registered trademarks of Penguin Random House LLC.

Visit us on the Web!
rhcbooks.com
BerenstainBears.com

Educators and librarians, for a variety of teaching tools, visit us at RHTeachersLibrarians.com

Library of Congress Control Number: 2021949804
ISBN 978-0-593-30248-4 (trade) — ISBN 978-0-593-30524-9 (ebook)

MANUFACTURED IN CHINA
10 9 8 7 6 5 4 3 2 1

One afternoon, Brother and Sister Bear were minding their little sister, Honey, down at the neighborhood playground. Many other cubs were there, too, with their younger brothers and sisters. They helped them play on the slides, the swings, and the seesaws. Everyone was having a very nice time.

Everyone was having a very nice time, that is, until the neighborhood bully, Too-Tall Grizzly, showed up with his younger cousin, Too-Small.

"Uh-oh!" said Brother to Sister. "Here comes trouble."

Brother and Sister had been through this before. Little Too-Small was just like his older cousin—a rough, rude bully.

At once, Too-Small started shoving his way past cubs who were waiting in line for a slide.

"Out of my way!" he said in his high little voice. He laughed as he zipped down the slide.

Too-Small did the same thing at the swings and the seesaws, pushing and shoving and bossing the other cubs around.

"Too-Tall!" said Brother angrily to the rude cub's older cousin.
"Can't you do something about this?"

Too-Tall shrugged. "I guess he's just a chip off the old block.
I taught him everything he knows."

"That's the trouble," said Sister. "He's just like you."

There was only one thing to be done.

"Come, Honey!" said Brother. "It's time to go."

Most of the other cubs did the same. There was no point in staying at the playground if Too-Small was going to ruin it for everyone. The older cubs took the younger ones by their hands and led them away.

Too-Small watched the other cubs leaving. His lower lip began to quiver, and his eyes filled with tears. He started to cry.

"WAAH!" he cried. "I don't have anyone to play with! Make them come back! WAAH!"

"What a racket!" said Too-Tall, covering his ears. He tried to calm his little cousin down. But Too-Small kept right on screaming.

"Wait a minute!" said Too-Tall, running after Brother, Sister, and Honey. "What's your rush? Hang around for a while. My cousin needs someone to play with."

"Nothing doing," said Sister. "No one wants to play with him. He plays too rough and rude. He needs to learn how to be fair to others."

"But," pleaded Too-Tall, "maybe he can learn. Maybe someone can teach him."

"Who?" asked Brother. "You?"

"Well, no," admitted Too-Tall. "I'm not good at that fairness stuff. But maybe you two could give him some lessons. You're a couple of sweethearts!"

"Well . . . ," said Sister, looking back at Too-Small screaming his lungs out, "it is a shame to leave him like that. Okay, we'll give it a shot."

So Brother and Sister calmed Too-Small down. They explained that if he learned to be fair to others, he would always have other cubs to play with. That made Too-Small happy.

When the other cubs saw Brother and Sister trying to teach Too-Small how to behave, they came back to help.

The older cubs taught Too-Small about taking turns, about not pushing and shoving, and about not bossing other cubs around. He soon got the hang of it and began playing nicely with the other cubs. Everyone started having a very pleasant time at the playground again.

"Hey, you guys!" said Too-Tall to Brother and Sister. "Thanks for helping me out with my little cuz here!"

"We didn't do it for you, Too-Tall," said Sister. "We felt sorry for him because no one ever taught him how to play nicely. Maybe you could take a few lessons from him now!"

"Heh! Heh!" chuckled Too-Tall, amused.

As the cubs left the playground and headed home, little Too-Small stood to one side.

"After you, cousin dear!" he told Too-Tall. Too-Tall was confused.

"Uh, how sweet!" replied Too-Tall. "Um, thank you?"

Brother, Sister, and Honey shook their heads. They didn't think old Too-Tall would ever get the hang of it.